FIN M'COUL

THE GIANT OF KNOCKMANY HILL

THE GIANT OF KNOCKMANY HILL

retold and illustrated by

TOMIE DE PAOLA

A TRUMPET CLUB SPECIAL EDITION

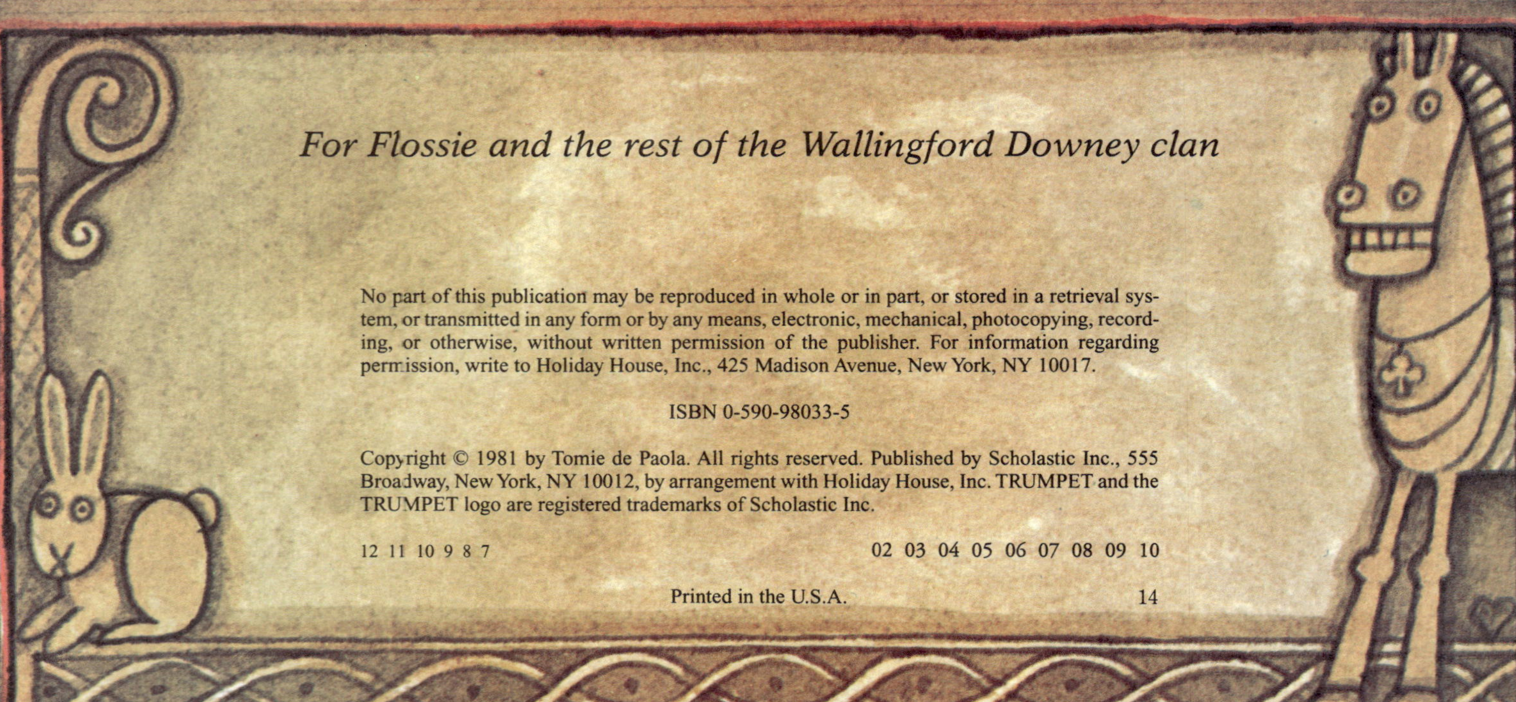

For Flossie and the rest of the Wallingford Downey clan

ISBN 0-590-98033-5

 Published by Scholastic Inc., 555 Broadway, New York, NY 10012, by arrangement with Holiday House, Inc. TRUMPET and the TRUMPET logo are registered trademarks of Scholastic Inc.

12 11 10 9 8 7 02 03 04 05 06 07 08 09 10

Printed in the U.S.A. 14

In olden times,
when Ireland's glens and woods
were still filled with fairies and leprechauns,
giants, too, lived on that fair Emerald Isle.

One of the finest of those big folk was Fin M'Coul,
who was wed to the lovely great lass, Oonagh.

They made their home on the top of Knockmany Hill.

Now, as any good giant,
Fin M'Coul had his work to do,
so he was often away from home.
Lovely Oonagh didn't seem to mind,
for there was plenty to keep her own hands busy.
Spinning, knitting, and even giving a pretty touch
to their great house.

Life was very pleasant indeed.

One morning,
when Fin M'Coul was busy
working with his kin
building a causeway to Scotland,
the word came that Cucullin was coming.

Cucullin was a giant too, and without a doubt the strongest in that part of the world. When he walked, the very earth trembled, and with one blow of his fist he had flattened a thunderbolt so it looked like a pancake. He was so proud of *that* feat, that he kept the thunderbolt in his pocket to show all just how strong he was.

Every giant in Ireland
had been given a good beating by Cucullin.

Every giant, that is,
except Fin M'Coul.
And Cucullin swore by the green
that he would never rest,
day or night, winter or summer,
until Fin M'Coul was added to his list.

So far, Fin had been smart enough.
He kept moving about whenever he heard
that Cucullin was in the neighborhood.

But this time, Cucullin was sure to get him.

So Fin left the causeway
and sped off for Knockmany Hill,
his house, and his darling Oonagh.

"Fin, m' love," said Oonagh
greeting him at the door,
"what brings you home so early from your work?"

"The chance to get a sight of you,
my sweet thing," said Fin.
Since he was as honest as the summer day is long,
he added, "And to keep out of the way of Cucullin.
He's after me!"

Oonagh soothed her husband.
She brought him his slippers
and lit a pipe for him.
She stirred up the peat fire so it would be cozy.
Then she set down a huge mug of stout
and cut a gigantic slab of soda bread for her dearie.

"Fin, husband of mine, enough is enough,"
said Oonagh as gently as she could.
"For years, you've been hikin' around
from one place to another to avoid this Cucullin.

"Why, you even built our house high on this windiest of hills so you'd be able to spy him comin'. You'll not get a moment's rest until you stand fast and face him."

"Aye, I'll be getting *plenty* of rest if I stand fast and he knocks me down. I don't have the heart to face a man who can make a young earthquake just with his walk and who carries around a flattened thunderbolt in his pocket just to prove his strength."

At that Knockmany Hill gave a little dance.

"He's coming!" said Fin,
his face turning a fine shade of pale green.

"Now hush," said Oonagh,
"and give me time to think.
Do you worry that I won't do all I can
to help you settle this matter once and for all?"

Oonagh then worked a charm
the fairies had taught her.
She took nine woolen threads,
each a different color,
and braided them into three braids.
She put one around her right arm,
one circling her heart,
and the third around her right ankle.
Now, nothing she did could fail.

Next, she sent around to all the neighbors
to borrow one-and-twenty iron frying pans.
She hid them in one-and-twenty loaves of bread
that she baked on the fire in the usual way.
She set them in the cupboard
with some bread she had baked the day before.
She then took a pot of milk
and made it into a fresh wet cheese
and put it along with some white stones
at the foot of the cradle she had made up.

"Now my darlin'," she said,
handing Fin some baby clothes.
"Put these on and do everything
just as I'm about to tell you."

"And remember," she said at the last,
"Cucullin's strength lies in the brass finger
he has on his right hand.
Now, quick, into the cradle because I hear
that man-mountain at the door."

"All right, woman,"
bellowed the giant at the door.
"Where's that coward, Fin M'Coul,
that I've been chasin' after, all this time?"

"Well, well," said Oonagh
with her sweetest smile.

"Now isn't that a shame.
Fin was off workin' on the causeway
when some important family affair called him away.
But he'll be home by tea time,
so why don't you just come right in and sit down."

Poor Fin trembled in the cradle.

"See this," Cucullin said,
pulling what looked like a pancake out of his pocket.
"THIS WAS a thunderbolt,
until I caught it and flattened it.
And that's what I'm goin' to do to Fin M'Coul, too."
"Tsk-tsk," said Oonagh.
"That may not be as easy as you think.
Fin M'Coul's a big broth of a man.
Why, take a look at our little baby
and you might be gettin' an idea
of the strength and breadth of Fin himself."

Cucullin peeked in the cradle.

"Chirrup," said the huge baby looking back at him.
"My," said Cucullin, "what a big boy!"

"While you're waitin',
why not have a bite to eat," said Oonagh.

She put some loaves of bread on the table,
along with a can or two of butter
and a pile of cabbages.

Cucullin, who was as much a glutton
as he was a bully,
popped a loaf into his mouth
and took a huge bite—
right down on one of the frying pans.
Clang!

"Yowl!" shouted Cucullin.
"What kind of devil's bread is this?
Here are two of my teeth out!"

"That's Fin's bread,
the only kind he eats," said Oonagh.
"Is it a bit too tough for you?"
"Too tough for me?" shouted Cucullin.
"I should say not. Just give me another."
Cucullin chomped into another loaf . . .
and, into another frying pan.
"I'll not have a tooth left in my mouth, woman.
There's two more out!"
Cucullin hollered even louder.

The baby began to holler too.
"Hungry, hungry, hungry."
"Ah, sweet dumplin'," said Oonagh,
and she handed Baby-Fin a loaf.
And because there was no frying pan in it,
Fin ate it right down.
"More," said the baby,
and he gobbled up another loaf.

"He seems a strong lad," said Cucullin, getting a little worried.
If this was the baby, the father must indeed be a bit stronger than Cucullin thought.
"Ah, yes," said Oonagh beaming.
"Why, instead of dollies, he loves to play with those white stones there in his cradle.
Show the nice man, baby dear."

Fin did as he was told.
He picked up a stone that was really the cheese
and squeezed all the water out of it
and popped it into his mouth and ate it down.

Cucullin was not to be outdone by a baby.

He grabbed a stone and squeezed.
He squeezed. And squeezed.
Squeeze as he might,
he couldn't get one drop of water out of it.
He popped it into his mouth and with a chomp,
there went the rest of his teeth.

The howl that came out of him
almost broke all the windows.
When he finally calmed down,
Cucullin said to Oonagh,
"What kind of teeth does that lad have?
They must be made of iron!
Let me see your choppers, baby."

At that,
Baby-Fin opened wide his mouth,
and Cucullin stuck in his brass finger—
the very brass finger
that was the secret of his strength.

With a strong bite,
Fin M'Coul bit the brass finger right off.
Then up Fin leapt
and began to pound the daylights
out of poor, weak Cucullin.

That was that.

Out the door went Cucullin, never to bother anyone, let alone Fin M'Coul, again.

"Tea's ready, m' love," said Oonagh, and Fin M'Coul sat down with the best giant wife in the whole world. And they lived a long happy life.

ABOUT THIS BOOK

Stories about the popular Irish giant, Fin M'Coul, have been handed down from generation to generation.

Perhaps Fin M'Coul is best known for the Giant's Causeway, the highway he built between Ireland and Scotland.

The encounter between the giant, Cucullin, and Fin at Knockmany Hill is one of the funniest of Fin M'Coul's adventures.

Details in the border art were inspired by early Irish jewelry and metalwork.

Tomie de Paola has chosen to use William Butler Yeats' spelling of Fin M'Coul.

This book was set in Aster and Solemnis types by Norwalk Typographers, Inc.

The drawings were done in colored inks
on Fabriano 140-lb. hand-made watercolor paper.